The Brothers' Promise

Frances Harber

ILLUSTRATIONS BY **Thor Wickstrom**

www.av2books.com

Your AV² Media Enhanced book gives you a fiction readalong online. Log on to www.av2books.com and enter the unique book code from this page to use your readalong.

Go to **www.av2books.com**, and enter this book's unique code.

BOOK CODE

J610482

AV² **by Weigl** brings you media enhanced books that support active learning.

First Published by

ALBERT
WHITMAN
& COMPANY
Publishing children's books since 1919

AV² Readalong Navigation

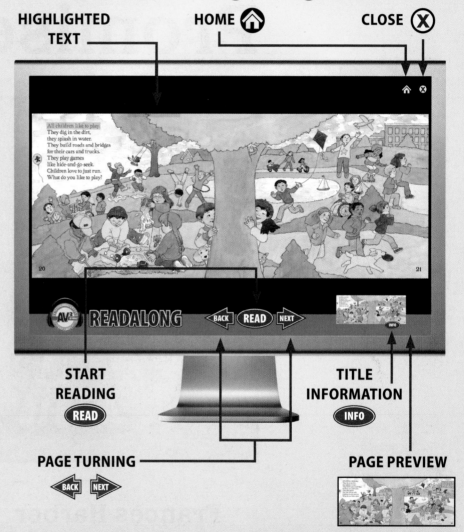

HIGHLIGHTED TEXT

HOME

CLOSE

START READING — READ

PAGE TURNING — BACK NEXT

TITLE INFORMATION — INFO

PAGE PREVIEW

Published by AV² by Weigl
350 5ᵗʰ Avenue, 59ᵗʰ Floor New York, NY 10118
Websites: www.av2books.com   www.weigl.com

Library of Congress Control Number: 2014937048

ISBN 978-1-4896-2311-9 (hardcover)
ISBN 978-1-4896-2312-6 (single user eBook)
ISBN 978-1-4896-2313-3 (multi-user eBook)

Printed in the United States of America in North Mankato, Minnesota
1 2 3 4 5 6 7 8 9 0 18 17 16 15 14

042014
WEP080414

Text copyright ©1998 by Frances Harber.
Illustrations copyright ©1998 by Thor Wickstrom.
Published in 1998 by Albert Whitman & Company.

For my sisters,
Mary and Terry, who are angels in my life.
—F. H.

In memory of my brother, Karl.
—T. W.

Once in yestertime there was a rich farmer. His name was Chayim, which in Hebrew means Life. Every seed that Chayim ever sowed burst into life.

Rows of beet leaves, fat cabbages, potato plants, and sun-kissed wheat filled his fields.

Chayim also raised two strong sons, Yankel and Josef. With their father's help, they, too, learned how to be good farmers. Chayim taught them that everything on earth has a season. A time to plant. A time to reap. A time to be born. A time to die.

One sad day, Chayim knew that his time had come. So he gathered his sons to his side for the last time. He made them promise to divide the land in half, to work together, and to always take care of each other. "Because when a brother helps a brother, the angels in heaven weep tears of joy," whispered Chayim just before he closed his eyes.

Yankel and Josef kept their promise to their father. But the two brothers were very different. Yankel married the tailor's daughter, and they had three fine children. After a hard day's work in the fields, Yankel liked nothing better than to be with his family, eating, singing, and playing his fiddle.

"Fiddle, schmiddle!" teased Josef one day. "Brother, is that all you can think of?"

Yankel pointed proudly to his happy children, who were dancing the hora on the tabletop.

"Josef, look! In the fiddler's house, everyone dances!"

But the dancing type Josef was not. He grew more like the beet; the best part was buried deep inside the ground.

Josef lived alone. On the other side of the farm, he built himself a simple house. When the day's work was done, Josef was happiest sitting quietly by a worn wooden table. There he studied holy books of wisdom like the Torah and Talmud.

"Too many books! It will take you a hundred harvests to finish them!" joked Yankel one night. "And why must you read so slowly?"

Josef explained, "When I pray, I pray quickly because I am talking to God. But when I read, I read slowly because God is talking to me."

Despite their differences, Yankel and Josef continued to be friends. They worked together, and the farm grew even richer.

While it is true that the earth has its seasons,
sometimes they get mixed up and trade places. And so it
happened one year that the sunny season came instead
of the rains.

All day long the sun glared. The earth dried up. Roots had nothing to grasp. Leaves shriveled and turned brown. For the first time, it looked like there would be no food from Chayim's farm.

One night, long after his wife and children were tucked in their beds asleep, Yankel stayed up. He played a sad tune on his fiddle. He was thinking about his brother.

"I have a wife and children to help me. Josef has no one. I wonder if he has saved enough food to last him through these hard times."

Silently, Yankel took a lantern and went down into the cellar. There he gathered beets, potatoes, cabbages, and wheat to pile into his wheelbarrow. Under a starry sky and across the empty fields, he pushed his load. In the distance, he could see one candle still burning in the window of Josef's little house.

"Josef must have his nose in a book. Good! I will slip into his barn and leave the food."

Tonight, Josef was not reading. A book was open, yet not a page had been turned. He was worrying about his brother.

"I am only one, but my brother has a wife and children to feed. If nothing on the farm grows, his whole family could go hungry!"

Josef thought and thought about this until his candle was just a flicker. Then he lit a lantern, went to his barn, and packed a wheelbarrow high with food. Josef pushed his heavy load across the fields towards his brother's home.

Everyone in Yankel's house was asleep. Even the fiddle. Josef crept into his brother's cellar and left the food.

The next morning, when Yankel went down into the cellar, he found he had exactly the same amount of food as he had had the day before.

"I thought I took food to my brother. Josef is right— I fiddle too much. My head is befuddled! I must do better tonight!"

When Josef went into his barn, he found that he had just as much food as yesterday.

"Didn't I take food to my brother? Yankel is right—I read too much. I am confusing everything. Tonight I will do better!"

That night, when the moon hung low in the trees,
Yankel heaped his wheelbarrow full of food and again
delivered it to his brother's barn.

Later, when the moon shone high in the sky, Josef, too, made another trip with a full wheelbarrow.

The next morning, both brothers found that not one potato or beet, kernel of wheat, or head of cabbage was missing.

"There is a little imp out there trying to trick me," declared Josef. "Tonight, in my brother's cellar, I will catch the little cheat."

"So! Now even the *ghosts* are worried about food! Why else would they steal it back, except to eat it later?" figured Yankel, squeezing a potato to see if it was still real. "Tonight, at my brother's barn, I will surprise the miserable old spirits and chase them back into the grave!"

Once again the brothers filled their wheelbarrows. Only tonight they both set out at *exactly* the same time.

In the distance each could see dark shadows dancing across the fields.

"Ha!" thought Josef. "The despicable
food-snatching imp!"
"Oho!" thought Yankel. "The greedy ghosts!"
Closer and closer the shadows loomed.

"The imp must be crazy. Why, he doesn't even try to hide his sneaky face!"

"Have these ghosts no shame? They don't even bother to flee!"

The brothers met neither imp nor ghost. In the middle of Chayim's farm, in the pale glow of moonlight, they met each other, face to face.

Each pushed a wheelbarrow full of food for the other. At once they understood what had happened, and they remembered Chayim's last words.

At that moment a spike of lightning split the night sky. When the brothers looked up, the heavens opened and poured out tears of joy that soaked the earth.